The Unrequited

The Unrequited

G.C. Bailey

G.C. Bailey

November 2020

Cover by Devotion/Shutterstock.com

Printed in the United States of America

First Printing: November 2020

Kindle Direct Publishing

ISBN 979-8-553-37853-0

"Lori"

The Unrequited

Grant Bateman took a long drag from his cigarette as he watched them dance. She was as beautiful as the first day he met her nearly twenty years ago. Lorene was laughing. Even from across the crowded dance hall, Grant could discern her laugh. His senses were always heightened when she was near. He could feel her presence often before he even knew she was there. The song ended and Lorene and Andy walked back to the table. Andy was a musician of some type; Grant didn't really care and had not inquired as to what instruments he played. As far as he was concerned, Andy was only there because he was smitten with Lorene. Everyone was-including Grant.

Grant and Lorene Walsh, "Lori" as he called her, first met at a friends' birthday party when they were young teenagers. They had hated each other when they first met, but childish ways soon gave way and they had become best friends by high-school. Now in their mid-thirties, it was as if they had never been apart. Grant had served as an artillery officer during the war. Though he had physically remained unscathed, his heart bore the scars of seeing killing. He might have gone mad if not for Lorene. Lorene-she was what he held on to and what kept him alive. She gave him purpose for living. She brought him back from the blackness within his heart and she had helped him heal. The scars were still there, but they had mostly healed. He stayed on for a while after the war ended and had been promoted to the rank of Major before deciding to leave the Army. He had planned to sail home until he received a letter from Lorene, informing him that she was travelling to Europe. He remained in Europe for her sake.

Lorene had married while Grant was away during the war. He had warned Lorene of marrying Robert, but she loved him and afraid of losing her friendship, Grant wished her his best. Grant's suspicions proved to be true. Robert, like all the men Lorene seemed to find, had been a scoundrel and they had divorced a few years back. Grant eyed Andy with suspicion. Sure he seemed all right, but Grant had a way of seeing through men that courted Lorene and viewed them all the same. To be fair, he knew no one would ever measure up to what she deserved- not even himself. Of course, Lorene knew Grant loved her. He had for years, but she never took Grant as a serious suitor. Grant blamed himself for that. He was too familiar to her. He had professed his love too many times. He was an open book and held no mystery to her. She knew he withheld no secrets from her. She knew things about him no one else did. He was dependable. He was steadfastly in love with her and Grant felt she knew he would always be there for her. He was proving her right by staying on in Europe.

"We're going to Paris next Tuesday," Lorene said as they approached the table.

"Oh? Just sight-seeing?" Grant asked absent-mindedly.

"Partly, but Andy has a friend who is playing at a club there Tuesday night."

Andy asked, "Why don't you tag along?"

Grant glanced at him. Either Andy didn't know Grant's feelings for Lorene, or he was goading him.

Andrew Strom, "Andy" as he was known, was slender with fine facial features-a far cry from the husky and square jawed Grant. Grant could see why Lorene fancied him. Grant didn't consider himself unattractive, after all, many women had complimented him on his features in no uncertain terms. Still, Andy was refined while Grant was rough and sinewy from years spent in the sun while in military service and hunting big game. He knew Andy was out of his league in the looks department, but there was

4

something about Andy that Grant didn't trust. Andy seemed smooth and cocky, with shifty eyes that seemed to follow every woman who walked by. This angered Grant. Grant had eyes only for Lorene, and he was furious anyone who had her attention would waste it by ogling other women.

"I imagine," he replied, "Lorene has seen enough of me for a while."

"Don't be silly," Lorene snapped.

"Alright. What time?"

Andy looked at his watch. "I think if we reach the station by 8:00 that will give us plenty of time."

"That's fine. I'll meet you there."

They asked for their checks and the waitress brought three bills. Grant watched as Andy reached in his pocket. Lorene also reached towards her purse but Grant knew she was being polite to Andy. Andy did not stop her, nor even protest that he pay for her meal. Grant was annoyed.

"Lori, the only thing you better be fetching from that purse is lipstick," he said sharply.

Lorene looked at him. She thought about scolding Grant for stepping in on her business but changed her mind. She liked being taken care of, even though it wasn't Grant's place to do so.

Andy picked up on Grant's move.

"Lorene, this is on me dear."

Andy paid for their meal then rose to leave.

Grant walked with Lorene to Andy's car. He hated to leave her, especially when she was with someone Grant wasn't comfortable with. It felt immoral to walk away from such a divine creation, but he didn't know what else to do. He was a simple man, but his emotions for Lorene always complicated things. He felt the urge, the obligation, and the necessity to protect her. This had caused him problems before when Lorene would tire of his hovering and remind him that she was not his to protect. Grant new she was right and he hated it. They said goodnight and Grant caught a taxi to his hotel.

Grant was fidgety the next few days as he waited to see Lorene again. He hadn't planned on staying on in Europe this long, but he couldn't leave her. An avid hunter, Grant passed his time visiting European firearm makers. While stationed in France, he had visited the facilities of firearm makers. Chapuis and Darne stuck out as his favorites there. He also had travelled to the Basque region of Spain to the famous gun-making town of Eibar and visited Grulla and Victor Sarasqueta. He especially liked the British firearms however, and had taken multiple trips to England. He visited the storefronts of Holland and Holland, John Rigby and Co.,

Purdey and Sons, W.J. Jeffery and Co., Westley Richards, Boss and Co., and C.G. Bonehill. He knew the models of each of their spectacular firearms. Although priced well beyond anything Grant could ever pay, that didn't stop him from admiring the craftsmanship that went into making each piece. He had been saving his money to buy an heirloom shotgun, and one day, while visiting W.J. Jeffery and Co., he spotted a used side levered side lock twelve gauge. Grant went to the counter and asked the gentleman if he could inspect it further. It balanced perfectly between his hands and was nearly the perfect length. Grant checked the price tag- £8,700. It was a little more than he had saved for, but he made a down payment with the promise to finish payment in three months' time. He had completed the purchase just before his discharge from the Army and went to pick up his new most prized possession. The man behind the counter watched Grant marvel at his new prize.

"It certainly fits you sir. Congratulations on your new purchase."

"She's beautiful! Thank you sir!"

"If I might suggest, perhaps you should wish you give your shotgun a name?"

Grant looked at the shotgun between his hands for a moment.

"That's a great idea. I think I'll call her Lori."

With that, they shook hands, placed Lori in the leather trunk suitcase, and Grant walked out of the store.

Grant was cleaning his shotgun when the phone in his hotel room rang.

"Hello."

"Hello Grant."

It was Lorene.

"Hi Lori! How are you?"

"I'm fine, thanks. Say, Andy is working on some music with his friends tomorrow and I thought maybe we could spend the day together."

"I'd love to Lori, but I am going to the shooting grounds early tomorrow and…"

"Oh, I'd love to see you shoot. May I come?"

Well if you'd like, sure. I'll come by and get you around 9:00. Is that ok?"

"That's fine Grant. I'll see you then."

Grant hung up the phone then returned to cleaning his shotgun.

"A day with two Lori's," he thought smiling to himself.

Grant came by Lori's hotel promptly at 8:45 the following day. It was a force of habit from so many years in the military to be fifteen minutes early to any engagement. Lorene wasn't ready, but Grant hadn't expected her to be. She never was. Grant waited in the lobby. Lorene came down just after 9:30.

"Ready?" Grant asked.

"Yes, sorry for the wait."

"You're worth waiting for."

Lorene smiled slightly.

"You're sweet."

They walked out of the hotel lobby and to Grant's car parked outside.

They were driving when Lorene noticed the trunk case in the back seat.

"Is that your gun?"

"Oh yeah, I forgot you haven't seen her yet. She is BEAUTIFUL."

"May I take a look at it?"

Of course! Help yourself.

Lorene got the case over the back seat with some difficulty.

"It's heavy!" she exclaimed laughing.

Grant had been laughing at her, amused with her struggle over the case.

"It's the case. The gun is light and perfectly balanced."

Lorene opened the top of the case.

"Grant! It IS beautiful!"

In a peculiar way, Grant looked at fine sporting firearms the same way that he looked at Lorene. He found them curvaceous, beautiful, potentially expensive, deadly, and magnificent to hold. Naming his shotgun after Lorene somehow made him feel more connected to her. He never allowed anyone to hold his "Lori," except now the one person he had named his gun in homage to- the flesh and blood Lorene. He felt proud seeing her marvel at the engraving and to know Lorene liked his purchase.

"Grant, you have to name her."

"I did!"

"Oh! What's her name then?"

Grant bowed his head and sheepishly told her.

"Lori."

"Oh Grant…thank you."

Her fingers lightly followed the pattern of the engraving on the sidelocks. She closed the lid and let the case rest in her lap. Grant noticed her fingers were slowly running along the profile of the case and he felt proud once again. Lorene understood Grant. Accepted him for who he was. There was no need for hiding behind an alternative personality pretending to be something he wasn't with her. With Lorene, Grant was able to truly be himself.

Grant and Lorene had a wonderful day together. He shot several rounds of various target presentations and then asked Lorene if she wanted to shoot her own namesake. Lorene excitedly shot a round of trap as Grant proudly watched his two Lori's perform in tandem. His gun was a bit long for her, but Lorene managed well enough. They had lunch on the shooting grounds and admired the scenery. Grant felt he got more out of the experience however, as Lorene added another level of beauty to the rolling hills surrounding them. That was the odd thing about Lorene; she never seemed aware of how beautiful she was. To Grant, her beauty was doubled because he saw her beauty that was within her as well as her outward beauty. Grant dropped her back off at her hotel at six that evening and walked her to the lobby.

"Thank you for coming today Lori."

"Grant, I had a wonderful time! Thank you for taking me with you. I would have been bored to tears just sitting in my room."

After they said their goodbyes, Grant walked to his car and returned to the hotel.

Grant was at the train station the following Tuesday promptly at 7:45. He purchased a coffee and a newspaper and sat on a bench. A few minutes later, he put the paper down and looked around. Lorene was there. He sensed her presence even before his eyes found her. He looked intently through the crowd. A hand touched the back of his jacket.

"Good morning Lori."

"How did you know it was me?"

"I could feel your…aura."

"You've always had that gift."

He turned around to look at her beautiful face and saw Andy standing beside her. His heart sank. He had forgotten about Andy.

"Good morning Grant!"

"Andy," was the only reply as they shook hands.

Lorene gave Grant a big hug. He hugged her in return. He could smell her Armani Code perfume, pleasant and sweet. She had always worn that brand of perfume and Grant associated the scent to her. He breathed it in deeply, relishing every molecule of her that engaged his olfactory system.

He willed his arms from around her.

The train ride to Paris was uneventful, but enjoyable. Lorene talked about back home and reminisced with Grant, and talked music, Paris, and future hopes and dreams with Andy. Grant was slightly agitated with their conversation, as he knew all of Lorene's hopes and dreams better than he even knew himself. He had been a student of Lorene from an early age. He got the sense that Andy believed her to fancy the city life, but Grant knew she loved and belonged in the quiet solace of the country. Andy seemed to have her all figured out, yet to Grant, Andy was lazy and had not taken the time to really know her at all. Andy was making Lorene fit into what he wanted her to be. Still, her voice was like a nightingale and both men enjoyed listening to her.

Once they arrived in Paris, the air was crisp and the city was bustling with activity. A new president had just been elected and there were people celebrating and marching in the streets. Lorene shivered, partly with excitement and partly because of the cool air. She pulled her fur coat around her tighter and grasped Grant's arm. He looked down at her and smiled deeply. He loved her excitement and her smile. He was glad he had come. They hailed a taxi and drove deeper into the city.

They visited the Louvre and Notre-Dame Cathedral, followed by lunch at *Café Les Deux Magots*. The chill in the air had gone, so Lorene removed her fur coat. Beneath her coat Lorene filled out a blue dress better than Grant had ever seen. A delicate necklace with small pendant of a white dress lay just above the V cut in the neck of her dress. Grant watched her intently but not with lust. In fact, Lorene's nakedness was sacred to Grant. She was angelic and he did everything he could to treat her as such. He desperately wanted her, but she was so much more to him than a beautiful body. She was everything. She was poetry in motion. She spilled onto the pages of his heart. Lorene caught Grant watching her but she didn't mind. She knew him. Knew he wasn't a cad. She smiled gently at him and pulled her dress up a little to cover her beautiful cleavage. Grant admired her for her modesty, though he dreamed of a day she wouldn't need to be modest in front of him any longer.

Club le Perroquet was a jazz club with a quaint vibe. Grant liked it far more than he thought he would. Grant loved music of course, but his life did not revolve around it. He often found musicians to be pretentious and he had always hated jazz. Tonight was different. Perhaps it was because they were in Paris, or maybe because Lorene was there, or maybe it was simply the alcohol. Whatever it was, Grant was enjoying himself. He felt happier than he had in a long time despite Andy's arms snaking around Lorene's waist like a serpent constricting its prey.

Grant asked, "Lori would you like another drink?"

"Yes, thank you Grant."

"For you a thousand times."

He walked up to the bar, ordered a whiskey for himself, a Kir for Lorene, and waited for the server to prepare the drinks.

A Parisian woman wearing a form fitting black dress approached Grant.

"You are American?" she asked lightly touching his hand.

"Yes ma'am."

"I thought so, you don't dress like a European."

"What's wrong with what I am wearing?"

"Oh nothing, nothing at all! Quite the contrary, I just noticed you look different…what you American's say rugged? Have you been in Paris long?"

"A little while now."

"Perhaps you would like someone to show you around? Show you a good time?

"Thank you ma'am, but I am with her."

He pointed to Lorene.

"Oh she is beautiful. But I do not think you are with her."

"No?" Grant asked.

"I think she is with the other gentleman. I also don't think you like that. You look at her with eyes of longing, but she is not yours."

"I'm the one getting her a drink."

"Yes, she replied. "Another reason you look different. She isn't yours but you are making love to her from afar."

Grant laughed.

"You picked up on all that from me buying a drink?"

"A woman can tell when a man is in love.

G.C. Bailey

The way you look at her is the way every woman wants to be looked at."

Grant blushed and looked at the floor. She had pegged him and he had no response.

The woman continued, "Perhaps you need someone to take your eyes away from her? A distraction maybe? She might even get jealous seeing you with another woman.

"But I am not with anyone else."

"You could be. I am Elise."

The woman was delicately playing with her necklace, moving it from side to side over her breasts.

Grant was not versed in the subtle flirtation of women. Some women had found it cute, but Elise was annoyed that their advances were met so flatly.

"Hello, I'm Grant."

Andy approached the bar.

"Grant, who's your friend?"

He looked Elise up and down.

"Well anyway, it is nice to meet you Grant," Elise said with her thick accent. She took her drink and sauntered across the room to a table. Andy watched her all the way to her seat.

"Whew, did you see that caboose?!"

He slapped Grant on the shoulder.

"Andy, shouldn't you be paying attention to Lorene?"

"Well sure, but a guy can get a look can't he?"

Grant was furious. And jealous. He had never seen another woman after he found Lorene whose love and affection was now being squandered by…by…he was so angry he couldn't even form a word low enough to describe Andy.

The server placed his drinks on the counter. Without saying anything, Grant took the drinks to Lorene.

"Here you are Lori, a delicate drink for a delicate flower."

"Thank you Grant."

Lorene took a sip. Grant couldn't help but look and admire her neck as she drank.

"Lori, come back to America with me. I'll take you away from here and take care of you."

"Grant, I came with Andy remember? Besides, we haven't finished our trip."

"He's no good Lori. I don't like him at all."

"Well that is no surprise, no one is ever good enough to you."

"That is probably true, but he really is scum."

Lori snapped, "You make awful quick snap decisions about people. You only met him two weeks ago."

"Lori, please listen. I am a man and I can tell if a man is no good."

"He's no good because he isn't you."

"Lori, I only want what's best for you. If

he was a good man, I'd be happy for you."

"Andy isn't perfect, but he is nice and we are very happy. Grant, we really are happy."

"Lori, are you trying to convince me of that or yourself?"

Lorene was about to say something but Andy returned to the table. He sat down next to Lorene and placed his arm behind her chair.

"What did I miss?"

"Nothing much," Lorene replied flatly.

Grant knew she was angry with him. The band began playing a slow tune. Andy asked Lorene to dance.

"I don't really feel like it right now."

Lorene was sulking now. Grant saw all her tell signs. She was shaking her leg. Her lips were pursed to the left side of her mouth and Grant could tell she was deep in thought. That was the thing about Lorene, she was a thinker while he was a doer. Grant knew he might have crossed the line asking Lorene to go away with him. He thought of blaming his brashness on the alcohol but he had meant what he said. He also knew Lorene knew he was serious. He would take her anywhere she wanted to go if she would just take his hand and let him lead her away.

They sat at their table a long time not talking. Finally, Lorene said, "I want to go to the hotel." Andy had been drinking quite a bit and was not ready to leave. Grant offered to take Lorene back to her room. Andy said that was fine and Grant fetched her coat. Grant walked Lorene outside and hailed a taxi. He opened the door for Lorene. She got in and told Grant she knew where the hotel was. She didn't need him to go with her. Grant heard in her tone she was telling him to go away. He paid the driver and watched Lorene ride away.

Grant wasn't sure what to do next. His heart told him to go after Lorene, but he didn't know if she really wanted him to stay away or if she wanted him to pursue her. He certainly wasn't going to go back and spend time with Andy. He decided to go on a walk and think. He walked for nearly two hours when he suddenly realized he had walked to Lorene's hotel. He hadn't even realized he was walking there. He went to the main lobby spotted Lorene sitting alone at a table. He softly approached her.

"Lori."

She had been crying. He could see the slight swollenness in her beautiful eyes.

She whirled around glaring at him.

"Why are you here?"

Grant stuttered. "I don't, I don't know. I wanted to fix things. I wanted to see that you were ok."

"I'm fine!"

"Sweetheart, you've been crying. Can we talk?"

Lorene paused a minute then said, "We can talk upstairs."

Grant followed Lorene to her room.

When he went in, the room smelled of the same sweet perfume. Grant closed his eyes and breathed in deeply.

"What do you want Grant?"

"I told you, I wanted to check on you."

"What were you thinking?!?! Why would you ask me to leave with you?!"

"I was thinking that I can make you happy if you'd give me the chance."

Lorene was nearly beside herself with anger and emotion.

"What do you want from me?! You stress me out! You push boundaries! You ask things of me that I can't give you! You're exhausting!"

She spun around and began to cry aloud.

"Lori, I only want you to be happy. If I knew you were better off without me in your life, I would walk away and never look back. I will always love you, but I would do it for your sake."

"You are STILL doing it! Don't ask me to make those kind of decisions!!"

Grant walked up behind her and gently but firmly placed his hands on the side of her arms.

"Lori, I am so sorry. I don't mean to do those things. I don't want to be those things. I want to make you happy."

"Do I look happy?!"

Grant didn't respond. He didn't know what to say or do. He was trying to reassure her. He wanted his presence to show Lorene that he would pursue her and be there when she needed him, but now he felt she despised him. Grant was scared. Few things scared Grant, not even war, but the busty little five foot four inches of creation standing there terrified him. He released her arms and took a step back.

"Lori."

"Grant please just leave. I can't take this tension, the constant chasing after me."

"Lori…"

"Just go! I'm begging you to please go!"

"As you wish Lori. I am sorry…for everything. I didn't mean for this to…"

"GO!!"

Grant reluctantly left. He was walking down the stairs when he met Andy. Andy would be there to comfort Lorene and it made Grant sick. Grant wanted to punch Andy, knock him down the stairs, and tell Andy what he really thought of him. They passed by without saying a word.

Grant gave Lorene some time before he tried to see her again. Eventually he decided to reach out to her and repair their friendship. His calls and letters went unanswered. She would not see him. One day, he ran into Andy at a café. They shook hands. Grant got right to the point.

"How is Lorene?"

"I think it's better if you stay away from her Grant."

This infuriated Grant. He and Lorene had been friends for twenty years. Despite his love for her, they had always been friends first. He valued her friendship more than anything.

"Andy, we are friends. Friends don't just leave- not real ones. I will never abandon her. She was the only one there for me after my car accident. She was there for me during the war. She was there after the war. I'll never ever abandon her."

"What if that is what she wants?"

"Andy, if not having me in her life made her life better, then I would walk away and never look back. I told her so. But I have to hear her say it."

"Well, I think you two have argued

enough."

"Andy, one should not measure a relationship by the lack of conflicts, but how those conflicts are resolved."

"Well my friend, you aren't resolving anything with Lorene. Get that through your thick skull."

Months passed. Grant was beside himself with worry. He had to fix his relationship with Lori. Unknown to Grant, Lorene and Andy were having problems of their own. Andy had told Lorene she was one in a million and began to show it. Lorene had caught him having dalliances with various Parisian women and each time he had promised to stop. At first, he blamed his lack of moral fortitude on alcohol, stress, and even immaturity. Then he began to blame Lorene for his reason for cheating. He told her that her nagging was making things worse. That if she could just be more understanding, he wouldn't feel the need to be comforted by someone else. Lorene began to think about

Grant. He was over protective, annoying, boyish in many ways, and utterly exhausting, but he was loyal. Still, her pride prevented her from reaching out to Grant. She didn't want Grant to know he had again been right about her choice of men. She tried to forgive Andy. Tried to work things out. She blamed herself and tried to be more like what Andy told her he wanted.

One day, Grant felt Lorene was near. Frantically, he looked around and saw her leaving a clothing store from across the street.

"Lori!" he yelled as he waived his hand at her.

Lorene looked at him then got in a taxi and sped away. Grant watched her drive into the distance, his hand still in the air. Lorene cried in the taxi. She wanted to go to Grant but she felt conflicted. She had wanted to run to Grant. She knew he would hold her and make her feel better. She knew Grant was the man she needed, but she couldn't give herself to him, not now. She realized again felt the painful sting of unrequited love. The kind of pain that burns from your heart straight down to your gut. The feeling of complete hopelessness. Only now, she realized how Grant felt towards her. The pain was palatable. Of course Grant did not know this. Lorene kept that part of her locked away from him. Grant saw her leave and he was broken. Completely and utterly broken. He had been a rock against the world. He had fought in two wars and his heart was scarred and heavy. But losing her wounded him in ways that wars never could. He booked a ticket to return to the United States the next day.

Grant's belongings were packed in trunk cases. He folded the letter in an envelope and placed it in his coat pocket. He took a taxi to Lorene's hotel and walked into the lobby. He walked to the reception desk and was about to give the clerk the letter when he spotted Andy drinking at the bar. He walked over and ordered a drink.

"Andy."

"You again."

"Don't worry, this is for the last time. I'm sailing home tomorrow morning."

"Good for you. And good riddance."

"Is Lori around?"

"She won't talk to you. She won't even talk to me. That's why I'm down here now drinking."

"What happened? Is she alright?"

"She's fine but nothing you're going to get involved in."

"Well, as a token of goodbye, will you give this to Lori?"

He retrieved the letter and handed it towards Andy. Andy looked at the envelope then slowly took it.

"Alright, as a parting favor, I'll see that

she gets it."

"Thanks. So long Andy."

Grant took a swig of his drink and walked out of the hotel lobby for the last time.

After he left, Andy looked at the envelope Grant had placed in his care. He opened the envelope and read the letter:

My dear Lori,

Please forgive me for any injustice I dealt you. I meant to do right for you but I suppose I only made things worse. I turned my best friend against me. Despite our ups and downs, despite that I love you, we have always remained friends. We were friends first. Even if you are never more than that, I value your friendship above all else. I am returning home and will not bring shame to you any longer. I wish you and Andrew the best. I mean that. You deserve the very best and so much more. It would mean the world to me if you came to see me off. You don't have to say a word. Just to see you there will let me know that things are well between us. All my love.

Grant had written many a correspondence letter, usually closing with *Sincerely* or *Best Regards*. But there was one valediction- one word that he reserved for only letters to her; letters he signed simply *Tenderly*. The letter never reached Lorene. Andy ripped it up, put it in an ashtray, and set it on fire.

The sound of the ship's low bellow echoed over the docks. Grant stood at the railing hopelessly searching for Lorene. She never came. He watched until the shoreline was well out of sight. He had come all this way; waited all this time for Lorene, but she couldn't even make the short drive to see him off. He retreated to his quarters defeated. Perhaps he could find a way to let go of Lorene. Perhaps he could find a new life in the United States. Maybe things would be better once he got home. Home. Home was with Lorene. He would never feel the same or be the same without her. Even the United States would feel like foreign soil without her walking the ground there. Grant looked around the room helpless. He saw his shotgun case on the floor. He opened the case and admired its beauty.

"Lori," he muttered under his breath.

He took his beloved shotgun out of the case and examined it closely. He took two 2-½ inch shells and rolled them between his fingers.

Andy and Lorene were silently eating breakfast.

Andy said, "Lori, let's go to Spain and get away from the bustle of Paris for a while."

Lorene sighed, "Don't call me 'Lori,' only Grant calls me that."

"That reminds me, he sailed back to the States this morning."

"What?!"

"He came to me yesterday and told me. He told me not to tell you, but I thought you should know."

"He wouldn't just leave without saying goodbye. That isn't Grant."

I'm awfully sorry darling. Perhaps he thought it would be better this way; that you could be happy without him in the picture."

"Oh yes Andy, and you have made me so happy with your infidelities! Grant will write or phone me once he arrives in New York. He would never just leave without saying goodbye or offering a reason for leaving so suddenly."

They finished breakfast in complete silence.

Lorene never received a call and no letter ever came from Grant. Grant never saw the shores of his homeland again. Passengers aboard the ship awoke one night to the sound of a gunshot. Some of the guests, who had been walking by, notified the crew that the sound came from Grant's room. When they broke the lock and rushed in, Grant lay on the floor in a pool of blood. His shotgun lay beside him. Clutched in his hand was a note, the ink smeared in blood. As they took his body away, the only word in the letter that could be read was *Lori*.

About the Author

Author G.C. Bailey is a US Army Field Artillery officer and veteran. His immersion in the profession of arms and lifelong passion for poetry and short stories lend an unparalleled authenticity to experiences in life; including love, loss, and combat. G.C. Bailey is a native of Statesboro, GA currently living in Oklahoma. He is an avid outdoorsman and spends most of his free time hunting, fishing, exploring, and writing. New to the writing field, his current writing has consisted a reflective hunting story for "Sporting Dog Journal" and poetry book *Of The Sea*.

Made in the USA
Columbia, SC
07 March 2023

13296821R00029